...Alison... was... brought up... ... ...
... ... She
spent three years... then did various jobs,
including... ... ... working at the
... ... pool at London Zoo.

Eventually Alison went back to College, and
found that school could be a lot of fun. When she
married and had three children, she stopped
teaching and wrote occasional pieces for the local
paper. Then, out with the pram one day, she met an
artist with four babies (she'd had twins twice). They
put together a story about a kid called Joe which
became a TV series. This led on to another series,
Trumpton, and then to a week of *Jackanory* stories.
Books followed, together with weekly stories and
pictures for children's comics.

Alison moved out of London with her family to a
derelict farm in Suffolk. After that there were more
moves, until she found her real home on the Isle of
Arran, where she still lives and works...

To Rod – and railways

ORCHARD BOOKS
96 Leonard Street, London EC2A 4XD
Orchard Books Australia
32/45-51 Huntley Street, Alexandria, NSW 2015
ISBN 1 84362 648 9
A paperback original
First paperback publication in 2004
Text © Alison Prince 2004
The right of Alison Prince to be identified as the
author of this work has been asserted by her in
accordance with the Copyright,
Designs and Patents Act, 1988.
A CIP catalogue record for this book is available from
the British Library.
1 3 5 7 9 10 8 6 4 2 (paperback)
Printed in Great Britain

Tower-block Pony

Alison Prince

ORCHARD BOOKS

CHAPTER 1

Our flat's on the tenth floor, and there's sky all round. If you want to see the ground, you have to stand close to a window and look down. We're on the edge of the town, so the view from my bedroom is all streets and houses, but if you go to the front of the flat where there's a balcony, things look a lot greener.

In the distance you can see the airport, where Mum works. She's on a check-in desk. That's where she and Dad met – not at the desk, I mean, at the airport. He bought her a coffee in the canteen and that was it.

Dad used to drive one of the tugs that back the planes out from the stand. He was mad about aeroplanes – he wanted to be a pilot, but he never passed the exams. Writing isn't his thing, he says. He's a long-distance lorry driver now, so he's away from home a lot. He goes to places like Germany and Spain.

I like looking out of my window at night. The traffic down there is a stream of red tail-lights going one way, white lights the other, like a moving map. And there's a railway line, too, though you can't see much of it.

I'm really into railways. Dad gave me this book with diagrams of the lines at big stations like Clapham Junction. You can trace the way the points have to be set so each train finds the right way through. I know the diagrams by heart now. I chalked the Waterloo one on my bedroom floor last year, but there was a bit of a fuss about that. Mum said, 'Dermot, really. Railways are all very well, I don't mind your model trains, but what on earth is this, we'll be treading chalk all over the flat. You can scrub it off, right now.' It took me ages.

My sister wasn't any help, of course. She put her fists on her hips and sighed, the way older sisters do. Her name's Maeve, and she thinks railways are boring, which shows what a ridiculous person she is. She's mad about horses. That's about as stupid as you can get, in the middle of a city where you never see a horse unless it's got a policeman on it.

Let's face it, my sister has always been bats. Ever since I can remember, she's been going on at Mum and Dad to move to a place in the country, with fields and a stable for a horse. 'We could have a farm,' she'd say. Never mind that Dad couldn't water a plant, let alone run a farm, or that Mum would freak out at the idea of turning a dear little pig into sausages. None of that mattered to Maeve. All she could think about was getting her hands on a horse. She wore boots all the time, and this stinky old jacket she found in a charity shop. She said it was a hacking jacket, whatever that is, and she carried lumps of sugar in her pockets in case she came across a needy horse. Which she never did. Well, not at first, anyway.

Her best friend is called Winnie. I thought it was a joke at first, because whinny is the noise a horse makes, but the pair of them looked down their noses when I laughed. They've got no sense of humour when it comes to horses.

Maeve was supposed to be in charge of me on the way to school and back, but I packed in sitting anywhere near her and Winnie on the bus. The pair of them talked non-stop about snaffles and bridles and stirrups, stuff like that. Tack, they called it. They showed each other pictures of horses they'd cut out of magazines, and cooed over foals and said things like, 'Look at the hindquarters on that chestnut gelding.' Even from the other side of the bus, I could hear them. It took real concentration on a shunting yard diagram before I could shut them out.

Then they found a horse.

I'm not kidding, they really did. There were a couple of small houses not far from our flat, left from where there used to be some sort of village before the estate was built, and one of these houses had a scrubby field beside it, with an overgrown hedge all round. We'd walked past it every day for ages, going to the bus and back, and there'd never been any sign of a horse – then suddenly there was.

Maeve and Winnie stopped dead. 'LOOK!' they shrieked. 'Oh, what a DARLING!'

I didn't think it was a darling. The horse was brown and white, except it was so muddy, it looked like brown and brown. It was standing by a rotten old shed in the field, rubbing its neck up and down against the doorpost. I thought the shed might fall down if it went on doing that, but I didn't say so. Maeve and Winnie hung over the gate and called and made clucking noises, and the beast ambled across.

Maeve's sugar lumps came in handy at last. She had to blow bits of fluff off them because they'd been in her pocket so long, but the horse ate them all the same.

'He's an Arab, isn't he,' Winnie said. 'You can tell by the fetlocks. He'll be a lovely mover.'

Maeve looked superior and said, 'Nah,

more like Connemara-cross-Dartmoor. Could be a trace of Arab I suppose,' she added, to make Winnie feel better. 'Just under fourteen hands, isn't he. More a pony than a horse.'

When the pony or horse had eaten all the sugar, they tried feeding it handfuls of grass, but it didn't like that so much and it went off back to the shed.

I was absolutely freezing because it was a cold day, but Maeve and Winnie wouldn't budge from the gate.

'Somebody needs to groom him,' said Winnie. 'Poor darling, just look at his coat.'

Maeve nodded and said, 'His feet are overgrown, too. He needs a trim.'

So they talked about horses' feet for another ten minutes.

I said, 'I'm going home,' and walked off.

'Wait!' Maeve shouted. 'You can't go alone, Mum will say I'm neglecting you.'

'Mum won't be in,' I said, 'she's on late

shift.' And I kept going. After all, I was nearly nine at the time, perfectly able to look after myself. Winnie and Maeve trailed along behind me, still talking about the horse.

'That shed must be ever so draughty,' said Winnie. 'It's an absolute wreck.'

Maeve nodded. 'He ought to have a New Zealand rug,' she said. 'But at least his coat hasn't been clipped, and if he's partly Dartmoor he'll be hardy.'

They were still going on about the horse when we reached our block of flats. We went up in the lift to the tenth floor and Maeve let us in with her key. Winnie came, too. She lives downstairs, but her mum never gets in until six, so she comes back with us.

'I wonder what his name is,' Maeve said.

Winnie suggested they could call him Patchwork. 'Because he's brown and white.'

Maeve wrinkled her nose. 'Boring,' she

said. 'If he's Connemara he'll have a real turn of speed. Let alone Arab. He needs a fast sort of name. What about Lightning?'

I thought that was ridiculous. I told them, 'Horses aren't that quick. Not compared with trains. Even Stevenson's Rocket went faster than a horse, and that was the first locomotive in Britain. 1829. It did twenty-nine miles an hour. It says so in one of my books.'

'Horses go faster than twenty-nine miles an hour, don't they?' asked Winnie.

''Course they do,' said Maeve, but she was looking thoughtful. 'You could be right. Rocket's a nice name.' She beamed at me and patted my head, though I ducked. Her hands smelt of horse. 'Aren't you clever!' she said. 'Yes, we'll call him Rocket.'

Mum came in about ten minutes later, so they told her all about Rocket, and the next thing I knew, Mum was going on about growing up in Ireland, and how the kids used to ride these ponies they kept on the waste land round the flats. I'd heard it all before, of course, about her begging her mum and dad to let her have a pony, only they never did. So she used to sneak rides on these ponies the other kids had.

When Winnie had gone home, Maeve sighed and said, 'Mum *couldn't* we move to the country? Or at least to a flat like in Ireland, with waste land round it?'

'No, me darlin',' Mum said with a return to her Irish accent. 'I told you before that we couldn't. Not for quite a while, anyway. And don't you go bothering your dad about it.'

'As if I would,' said Maeve.

She may be batty, but she knows Dad has a short fuse when it comes to the subject of living in the country. Last time she mentioned it, he roared, 'Get this through your head, Maeve,

THERE'S NO WORK IN THE COUNTRY. And I never want to hear horses mentioned again, RIGHT?'

And Maeve had looked at him and said, 'Right.'

CHAPTER 2

After they found Rocket, Maeve and Winnie were worse than ever. They went to see the horse every day after school, and hauled me along as well. I wanted to go home on my own, but Maeve wouldn't hear of it. She said she was responsible for me. I said if I froze to death beside the field, she'd be responsible for that, too, but she didn't seem impressed.

She and Winnie were sure the horse was hungry, so they fed it with stuff they carted about in their school bags. Maeve was always sneaking apples and carrots and crusts of bread out of the flat. Not just crusts, either. She picked up half a loaf one morning. Dad was there, packing his zipper bag to go off and drive a lorry somewhere, and he said, 'What are you doing with that?'

'Um − sandwiches,' Maeve said. She's always been a quick thinker.

Dad closed his eyes as if he was praying for patience, then said, 'Maeve, you and Dermot get dinner money. I'm the one who takes sandwiches, OK? So put that loaf back on the bread board, right now.'

'And get the cheese out of the fridge, there's a good girl,' said Mum, who had jumped up from the table to fish in the drawer for a plastic bag. 'Your dad'll be needing food for his journey, heaven knows when he'll next get a proper meal, these transport cafes, I don't know, nothing but fried stuff.' She looked at Maeve in a meaning sort of way and added, 'If you're wanting sandwiches, darling, let me know the day before and I'll get extra bread.'

'Thanks,' said Maeve. She and Mum smiled at each other, and I knew what they meant. Extra bread for the horse.

I felt ashamed of the pair of them, but I couldn't say anything. Dad glanced at me, rolling his eyes as if to say, 'What are they like?' I just shrugged and made a face.

A few days later, just after we'd picked up the kids from the next estate past ours, the school bus came to a sudden stop outside some shops. I went on reading my railway book, thinking the hold-up was just a traffic jam. Then I noticed there was a lot of noise going on. Cars were hooting and people were shouting and laughing, and there was a big crowd outside a greengrocer's shop. I stood up to see what they were looking at. Everyone else in the bus had stood up as well, pushing and shoving to get to the windows on the pavement side, so I had to do some pushing and shoving myself.

The driver turned round and shouted, 'Sit down, you lot, it's just a horse.'

My heart sank.

'A HORSE?' shrieked Maeve and Winnie. 'WHERE?'

They rushed to the front of the bus and stared out. I shut my eyes and shook my head like Dad had done when Maeve was going on about sandwiches. It would be Rocket, of course – had to be. There are no other horses living nearby, or Maeve would have known about it. I climbed on the seat behind the driver so I could see over the heads of the crowd. People were waving their arms and shouting and sure enough, a brown and white backside and muddy tail stuck out from among them.

'He's eating all the veg!' Kevin Dobb said. 'The shop bloke's doing his nut, look!'

He was right. As the crowd shifted around, I saw that Rocket was munching his way through the stuff on display outside the greengrocer's shop, and the greengrocer was not at all happy. He was walloping Rocket with a chewed-looking head of celery.

Maeve and Winnie were frantic. 'You've got to let us out!' Maeve screamed at the bus driver, 'That pony's OURS!'

Kevin said, 'Go on, you haven't got a pony.'

'Yes, we have,' said Winnie. 'You don't know, so shut up.'

Maeve was still shouting at the driver. 'He might be killed, there's lorries and things. Open the DOOR!'

And amazingly, the driver did.

Maeve and Winnie hurled themselves out, and I went as well. It seemed a better idea than going to school – I had a maths test that morning.

The driver shut the doors behind us to keep the rest of the kids in, and shouted through his window, 'I'm not waiting! If you're late for school, it's your own fault.'

We didn't answer. The girls were cutting through the crowd like guided missiles, and I was close behind them.

Rocket had his head in a sack of Brussel sprouts. Maeve bent down and stroked his ears. 'Darling!' she said. 'Are you all right?'

'I'll give him darling,' said the greengrocer. 'He's eaten half a sack of sprouts and five kilos of carrots, and just look at my Golden Delicious. Ruined. Not to mention the cabbages.'

'I expect he was hungry,' said Maeve.

The greengrocer's face turned a darker shade of purple. 'Oh, charming! If this is your blasted horse, why don't you feed it?'

'He's not exactly—' began Winnie. But the greengrocer had heard enough.

'GET THIS ANIMAL OUT OF HERE!' he roared. 'RIGHT NOW.'

'OK, OK, we're going,' said Winnie. She and Maeve tried to haul Rocket's head up from the sack, but he wouldn't budge. He didn't want sugar lumps, either – I suppose he liked the sprouts better.

'We've nothing to lead him with,' Maeve said. 'We need a halter,'

A man in the crowd said he had a tow-rope in his van.

'Oh, yes, please,' said Winnie. So he went and got it, and hacked a long bit off.

The rope was too thick and hairy to make into a halter, so the girls just tied it round Rocket's neck. They both hauled and made encouraging noises, but the pony wouldn't move. He leaned back with his head stuck out as if the girls were trying to pull it off, and made a strangled kind of coughing noise. Maeve and Winnie couldn't shift him, you'd have thought his feet were super-glued to the ground. Everyone heaved and shoved, but he stayed exactly where he was, and as soon as the girls slacked the rope a bit, he put his head back in the sprouts sack and went on eating.

I was still holding my railway book, so I

went round to his front end and thumped his nose with it.

The result was amazing. Rocket snatched his head up and barged off, scattering bits of sprout and dragging Maeve and Winnie with him. He nearly scattered an old lady and her wheelie bag as well, but she moved surprisingly fast.

We hurtled along the pavement. People were shouting after us, but we couldn't stop.

'Get in front of him!' Maeve gasped. 'Wave your arms or something!'

Did she mean me?

Yes, she did.

'Go on, Dermot!' she yelled. She and Winnie were hanging onto the rope, trying to slow the pony down.

I put on a turn of speed, but Rocket was travelling so fast, I couldn't get ahead of him. Then he came to a supermarket car park and shot off into it. There were only a few cars in there as it was quite early, but one of them hooted and that seemed to startle him. Just for a moment, he braked.

I still think I was an absolute hero. I got in front of Rocket, opened my railway book and pushed it in his face so he couldn't see where he was going. He staggered a bit and almost knocked me down, then turned his head sideways and started off again.

'Keep him turning!' yelled Maeve, and for the next few crazy minutes, the girls and the horse went round and round in circles in the car park while one or two drivers shouted encouragement. At last Rocket slowed down and stopped. I think he'd run out of breath. He wasn't the only one.

'Whew,' said Maeve. She and Winnie were panting, too. 'Well done, Dermot.'

I felt quite pleased, really.

CHAPTER 3

We started out again with Rocket. I walked in front of him, holding up the railway book in case he thought of bolting off again. The girls were on either side of him, hanging on to the rope round his neck, and we got him all the way to the field without any bother.

Winnie said, 'The gate's locked!'

She was right. The chain that held it shut was still in place, with a heavy padlock hanging from it as usual.

I wondered for a mad moment if the real Rocket had been in the field all the time and we'd got some other horse, but Maeve said, 'He must have broken through the hedge. You two hold him here and I'll go and look.'

She was back quite quickly. 'Found it,' she said. 'Come and see.'

We all went and looked at the gap in the hedge, taking Rocket with us. There were lots of broken twigs where he'd pushed through, with brown and white hairs caught up in them.

'If we put him back in, how can we stop him coming out again?' asked Winnie.

Maeve frowned. 'Perhaps we can mend it,' she said.

But we all knew we couldn't. We'd have needed something solid, like a pallet, and a lot of rope or wire, and we didn't have anything.

I said, 'Perhaps we can ask someone.'

We looked up and down the road. Cars went past, but there weren't any people on foot.

'We'll have to go to the house,' said Maeve, 'and tell his owner. It's a woman called Mrs Rix — Mum found out at the paper shop.'

I stared at the red brick house that stood beside the field. Bricks, I thought. Rix. They seemed to go together. And yes, the bricks woman would fix it. In two ticks. Box of tricks. Oh, shut up.

'But what if she can't mend the hedge?' Winnie was wailing. 'Rocket will get out again.'

'And she might decide she can't cope with him and sell him,' Maeve said gloomily. 'I mean, we know she's a hopeless owner.'

'That would be awful!' Winnie was almost in tears. 'We'd never see him again. What are we going to do?'

It was a silly question. 'We've got to ask Mrs Fixit,' I said. 'She might be OK.'

Maeve didn't quibble about the name. 'Right,' she agreed. 'Come on.'

We led Rocket round to the house and up the garden path. It wasn't much of a garden, all long grass and dandelions. It looked like Mrs Rix wasn't the practical sort, I thought – at least, not when it came to lawn-mowing.

Maeve banged on the front door and Rocket ate a few weeds. Maeve banged again. And again. Then she turned and looked at us.

'There's nobody in,' she said, though we knew that already.

'What are we going to do?' Winnie asked again, and I must admit, I couldn't think of an answer.

'Only one thing we can do,' said Maeve. 'We'll have to take him home.'

Winnie gawped at her. 'You mean up to the flat?'

Maeve said, 'There's nowhere else, is there? It won't be for long, only until we find Mrs Rix. Mum says lots of people in Dublin have ponies in their flats.'

'That's just one of her stories,' I said. Mum's stories were great, but I was never sure if they were actually true. 'And anyway, this isn't Dublin.'

'Shut up, Dermot,' Maeve said, and Winnie added, 'It's nothing to do with you.'

I wasn't sure about that. If Dad found out we'd had a pony in the flat, he'd go ballistic, and I'd be in trouble, same as the girls. But Dad was driving a lorry to Spain, and he wouldn't be back until the weekend. And whatever happened, I'd rather be here than at school, doing a maths test. So I shut up.

We got Rocket back to our block of flats without too much bother, but he wouldn't go in the lift. Maeve and Winnie tried pushing and hauling, one of them at one end and one at the other, but he rolled his eyes and laid his ears back, and went completely stiff, like he was a piano or something. I said we should put him on roller skates, but the girls didn't think that was funny. I took my thumb off the Doors Open button while I reached for his rope to help pull him into the lift, and the doors slid shut with me inside.

I pressed Doors Open again but the lift had started, and I was on my way to the twelfth floor. I got out there, and a family with lots of children and a buggy got in. With that lot inside, the lift was too full for me to get back in as well, and in any case I didn't want to admit I'd come to the twelfth floor by mistake, so I ran down all the stairs. There were twenty-four flights, two to each floor.

When I got back to ground level I couldn't see Rocket or the girls. I found them on the bit of grass behind the garages where it says No Ball Games.

'Have they gone?' asked Maeve.

'Who?'

'That lot with the buggy and the kids. They came out of the lift and asked a lot of silly questions about Rocket. We had to pretend we were going somewhere else. That's why we're round here.'

'Oh, I see. Yes, I think they've gone. I didn't see them.'

'Well, go and make sure,' said Maeve. 'Shout if it's OK, and we'll try again.'

'Right.'

I went back to the lift, but it wasn't OK. Gammy Sam was there, leaning against the wall and singing *The Wild Colonial Boy*. We call him Gammy Sam because he limps. He says he's got a gammy leg. Most of the time he's in the pub, but when he isn't, he walks about, singing.

When he saw me he stopped in the middle of his song and put his head on one side to stare at my railway book, which was still under my arm. This made him lose his balance a bit and he nearly fell over, but when he'd got things under control again he said, 'Now, there is a mag-nif-icent book.' Gammy Sam likes long words. He says them kind of slowly.

I showed him a page or two, and he thought it was great. He started on about the Good Old Days of Steam. I ought to have stopped him really, but I got interested. After a bit, Maeve put her head round the corner. She rolled her eyes in dismay when she saw Gammy Sam, and I gave her a helpless look, even if it was partly my fault.

Maeve disappeared again, and I heard her say to Winnie, 'Keep him there for a minute.' Then she approached on her own and asked Sam, 'Are you going up in the lift?'

'I might,' said Sam, 'or there again, I might not.' He thought about it for a moment, then he turned to me and said, 'Is this your sister?'

I admitted that it was.

Sam shook Maeve's hand politely. 'We were talking about en-gin-eering,' he said. 'And the glories of the iron horse.'

Maeve looked at him as if he was mad. 'Horses aren't iron,' she said.

Sam and I tried to explain, but I could tell Maeve wasn't listening. 'We'll just have to go for it,' she muttered to me. Then she turned her head, stuck two fingers in her mouth and gave a piercing whistle. I've always wished I could do that.

Winnie must have been waiting for the signal, because she came round the corner at once, with Rocket.

'Now, there's a handsome pony,' said Sam, not seeming much surprised. 'Bee-oo-tiful.' He lurched towards Rocket and patted him.

I got in the lift and made sure I kept the door open, and Maeve asked Sam, quite casually, 'Will you give us a hand to get him in?'

'Sure I will,' Sam said. 'Ab-so-lutely.'

Maeve and Winnie came into the lift and hauled, and Sam shuffled round to Rocket's back end, then gave him such a slap on the rump that he shot into the lift before he'd even thought about it. The door slid shut, and up we went. I could hear Gammy Sam shouting something as we left him behind, but after a floor or two, it faded.

Unfortunately, the lift didn't agree with Rocket's stomach, or else he'd eaten too much of the greengrocer's stuff. He lifted his tail, and out poured a huge amount of horse-poo. It smelt amazingly powerful.

'Fwoaaarrrgh!' I said. 'That's disgusting!'

'Poor darling, he's upset,' said Winnie.

'Probably motion sickness,' Maeve agreed. 'Remember how I used to get sick in the car?'

'Don't,' I said. What with the smell in the lift, Maeve being sick in the car was the last thing I wanted to think of. We reached our floor and the doors opened.

I pointed to the steaming pile and asked, 'What are we going to with that? We can't just—'

'Clean it up later,' said Maeve, and clucked at the pony. 'Walk on – good boy.'

Surprisingly, Rocket came out of the lift at top speed. Then he stopped dead, and we had another tricky moment getting him into the flat.

'Try him backwards,' said Maeve. 'Do your book trick, Derm.'

She and Maeve turned Rocket round so his tail end was towards the door, and I opened the railway book in front of his eyes. It was beginning to look a bit battered, but I couldn't argue – it was in a good cause. Rocket backed away from the book and into the flat, and we all crowded in as well and shut the door.

'Brilliant!' said Maeve. 'We've done it.'

CHAPTER 4

Rocket charged towards the kitchen, but we reckoned that wasn't a good idea.

'Get him in my bedroom,' Maeve gasped. 'Come on, Rocket – good boy.'

She and Winnie pushed and hauled the pony in through her door. Maeve's room is quite small, and it's full of clothes and stuff so it looks even smaller. Rocket only just fitted between the bed and the dressing-table, and he pushed at her TV set with his nose and almost knocked it over. Maeve unplugged it and started frantically grabbing CDs and magazines off the floor from under Rocket's hooves – it was the first bit of tidying she'd done for years. Mum used to go on about it, but she gave up.

Winnie said, 'It's not very comfortable for him. He needs some straw.'

'They sell it in the pet shop,' said Maeve. 'You'll have to go and get some. Take my bike, it's in the hall.'

'I can't carry a bale on a bike,' said Winnie.

'You don't have to get a bale. They sell it in plastic bags, for guinea pigs and things. Bring as many as you can.' Maeve was fishing in her purse. 'Here. Get some pony nuts, too. And some hay. That'll be in bags, as well.'

'But—'

'Go *on*.'

Maeve can be really bossy when she likes, so Winnie gave her a helpless look and collected the bike from where it leaned against the wall. I opened the door for her, keeping one eye on the pony in case he tried to bolt out – but he didn't. Maeve had both arms round his neck.

Winnie said, 'See you later,' and pushed the bike towards the lift.

Maeve let go of the pony. 'I think he's thirsty,' she said to me. 'Can you fill the washing-up bowl?'

'OK. You want it in here?'

'Yes, of course,' said Maeve. 'We'll put it on a chair so he can reach it. Like in a proper stable – they always have a drinking bowl at about head height. Get on with it.' She pulled a T-shirt from under one of Rocket's feet and tried to smooth it out.

I felt my insides turn over while I ran water into the washing-up bowl. What if Dad came home while the pony was still here? It didn't bear thinking about. But he wouldn't – no, we'd be all right. Today was Thursday, and he usually came back from a trip abroad on a Saturday. That was two whole days from now, a bit less if he arrived on Saturday morning. We could get rid of the pony by then, couldn't we? No choice about it – we *had* to get rid of him by then.

I carried the bowl into Maeve's room and found her trying to stop Rocket from pulling her pictures of other horses and ponies off the wall. She said, 'Take the magazines off that chair, look.'

I put the bowl of water down on the floor while I shifted the magazines – and of course the stupid animal put his foot in it and spilt the lot.

We'd only just finished mopping up and giving Rocket some more water, in a bucket this time, tied to the chair with a bit of string, when the doorbell rang.

A man in a warehouse coat with PETWORLD written on it was standing outside with a bale of straw in one hand

and a bag of pony nuts over his shoulder. He was grinning as though he found something very funny. Winnie was getting the bicycle out of the lift, but she was in a bit of a muddle because of the bags of hay on the handle-bars. Someone I couldn't see was shouting something from inside the lift. Whoever it was sounded very cross.

Winnie shouted back, '*All right*. We'll clean it up in a minute.' She hauled the bags of hay off the bike and said, 'Here, Dermot, take these in.' I went out to help her. She looked very flustered.

'Where's this pony, then?' asked the Petworld man, still grinning.

Neither of the girls answered. Maeve took the bale of straw from the man and dumped it on the hall floor, and told him, 'You can put the nuts down there, too.' She stood back while he did that, and Winnie and I slid past with the bike and the hay, then Maeve said to the man, 'That's all, thank you.'

'Go on,' said the man. 'Let's have a look at him.'

'He's not here,' said Maeve.

The man laughed and said, 'Who're you kidding? What's all this hay and stuff for, then?'

'Um – it's a gerbil,' Maeve said wildly.

'You're telling me a gerbil did all that in the lift?' said the man. 'Wow, some gerbil – his mother must have been an elephant. You ought to put him on TV, love, make your fortune.'

'Sorry, I'm busy,' said Maeve, and somehow she managed to push the man outside and slam the door. He was still laughing. Maeve turned to Winnie and said, 'You're such a prat, Winnie – why did you tell him?'

'It wasn't my fault,' Winnie protested. 'He said straw was much cheaper by the bale and it didn't matter if I couldn't take it on the bike, he'd deliver it in the van, and what was my address. I didn't tell him,

Maeve, honest I didn't, I said the bike was OK, but Mrs Ebberly was in there. You know who I mean? She lives downstairs, she's got those twins with the hamsters. She's friends with my mum, I don't know why Mum likes her because she's absolutely horrible, but she knows we're in the same block. So she told the Petworld guy, and he bunged the stuff in his van and said, "Get in, I'll run you both home." I had to sit on Mrs Ebberly's knee because she took up the whole seat, you know what a size she is. It was totally yukky.'

'You didn't have to let him come up here,' said Maeve.

'I couldn't stop him,' Winnie argued. 'When we got out of the van there were all these people standing round the lift, making a fuss about the poo, and Gammy Sam was there, telling them we had a horse upstairs.'

'Oh, great,' said Maeve. 'Just our luck.

OK, it wasn't your fault.'

'That's what I'm telling you,' said Winnie. She had to raise her voice a bit, because someone was ringing the doorbell and banging on the knocker.

'If that's the Petworld man, he's not coming in,' said Maeve. 'Dermot, where are the scissors?'

'Scissors?' I thought for a wild moment she was going out there to attack anyone who said a word about her precious Rocket.

'To cut the bale string,' Maeve said. 'What did you think?' Then she guessed what I'd thought, and got the giggles. 'You're such a nutter,' she said. The three of us sat on the bed and fell about laughing, and Rocket nosed at us and dribbled water all over my school shirt because he'd been drinking from his bucket. The banging and ringing went on, but we didn't take any notice.

Winnie found the kitchen scissors and

cut the strings on the bale. The straw kind of exploded all over the place – the next minute, we were knee-deep in it. Rocket started pushing it about with his nose, and Maeve said, 'I expect he wants some hay.' She ripped open a bag.

'We haven't got a rack or anything,' Winnie said, 'what shall we put it in?'

'We'll use another chair,' said Maeve. 'Dermot, can you get one?'

I fetched a chair from the kitchen. Most of the hay fell off it, but Rocket didn't mind – he got stuck into it straight away. He was a very untidy eater, I thought. The ringing and banging was getting more frantic.

'They'll have to wait,' said Maeve. She was struggling to get the stitching on the sack of pony-nuts undone.

I told her, 'If you pull the end, it'll run right along.' I knew, because I'd seen Kevin open a bag of cat litter when I was at his place.

'Go on then, clever clogs,' said Maeve. 'You do it. I'll get something to put them in.'

She came back with a pie-dish just as I'd ripped the stitching undone. I tipped some nuts into it, but the sack was heavier than I thought, and the stuff went everywhere.

'He mustn't eat all that, he might get colic,' Maeve said, and started grabbing up handfuls from among the assorted stuff on the floor.

Winnie was looking worried about the noise at the door. 'I expect they're fussed about the lift,' she said.

'Oh, all right,' snapped Maeve. 'Don't nag.'

'But we'll have to clear it up,' said Winnie. 'What can we put it in?'

I'd been thinking about this. 'Bin-bag,' I said, and went to get one.

'And a shovel,' Winnie shouted after me.

There didn't seem to be a shovel. We couldn't find anything bigger than a fish-slice, and I wouldn't let them use that.

'Perhaps the people outside have got one,' said Maeve.

Winnie shook her head. 'I doubt it,' she said. 'Come on, Maeve, we'll have to get out there or they're going to murder us.'

So we opened the door.

In spite of all the noise, it was only a small crowd out there, and they were all children. They didn't want to murder us. They just wanted to see Rocket. One little girl asked, 'Can we ride him?'

'Not just now,' said Maeve. 'Come back in about ten minutes. We've got some mucking out to do first.'

The little girl nodded and said, 'You mean the lift. We'll help, if you like.'

The lift had gone to the ground floor. We pressed the button, lots of times, but it didn't come up.

I said, 'Someone's holding the door open.'

'Down the stairs, then,' said Maeve. 'Come on.'

It seemed to be my day for running down stairs, but at least there were only twenty flights this time. The door was open, like I said, with a boy leaning against it, and a man was shovelling the last of Rocket's poo into a wheelbarrow. He pointed at it and asked, 'Your horse?'

'Um – not really,' Winnie admitted. 'We're just looking after him.'

'If he does any more, can I have it?' asked the man. 'I've got an allotment, see, and this stuff's great for runner beans.'

'Oh, yes, you're welcome,' said Maeve. 'We're on the tenth floor – you can come up and collect it any time.' Like I said, she's a quick thinker.

'Never mind about him and his beans,' said a large women who was watching. 'You want to get that lift scrubbed out.'

'That's Mrs Ebberly,' Winnie muttered in my ear.

I had to admit, the lift was very stinky. Although the man had shifted the muck, the floor was in an awful state, and the walls weren't too clean, either.

Maeve said, 'We'll have to go up and get the cleaning stuff.'

'Don't you keep the lift up there,' Mrs Ebberly warned her. 'People need to use it. I'll be watching.'

I don't know how many times the lift went up and down with us in it, mopping and scrubbing while people got in and out. The other children tried to help, but they got in the way, really. Mrs Ebberly was watching, like she said, but at least she let us come in to her flat for clean water. We were using Rocket's bucket because it was the only one we had, and Maeve was in a fret in case he needed another drink.

As we went up again, she said thoughtfully, 'You know, keeping Rocket in our flat could work quite well. Once we get him used to the lift, we can take him out and ride him every day. I'll muck out my room each morning and the man with the runner beans will take the stuff away.'

For a moment, I forgot about Dad and took this mad idea seriously. 'Oh, yes?' I asked. 'And where are you going to sleep?' I had a nasty idea what the answer would be.

'I'll share your room,' she said. 'You've got bunk beds in there, I can go on the top one.'

'No way,' I said. Maeve lives in a total tip and I like things tidy. 'I'm not having you in my room.'

'But it's an emergency,' said Maeve.

I said an emergency couldn't go on and on, but she didn't seem to take the point.

We were still arguing about it when the lift arrived at the ground floor and its doors slid open. Quite a crowd of grinning people had gathered, and Mrs Ebberly was telling someone, 'Yes – a horse. You should see what it's done to the lift. And it's up there in your flat.'

I thought I was going to die. The woman she was talking to was Mum.

CHAPTER 5

I smacked my forehead with my hand – of course, she was on early shift. With all the fuss about Rocket, none of us had remembered.

Mum looked thunderous. She came into the lift with its wet floor that smelt of disinfectant, and the doors slid closed behind her.

'Oh, very funny,' she said as we stood there with the bucket and mop and cleaning cloths. 'Have the lot of you gone completely mad?' She didn't wait for an answer. 'What on earth are you thinking of? This isn't a flaming zoo, there's barely enough room in our flat for the four of us, you know that. When you wanted a cat, I told you, we don't have room for it, what with its saucers and its litter tray, and you seriously imagine we can have a *horse*? Well, you can forget you even thought of it. He's going right back where he belongs, straight away.'

'But he might have been *killed*, Mum,' Maeve said desperately. 'He'd broken out of his field and he was running about in the road with all the traffic.' I thought this was going a bit far, but I didn't say so. 'And we tried to find Mrs Rix,' Maeve rushed on, 'only she wasn't there. I was going to look up her number and phone her, but I haven't had a minute, what with the lift and everything.'

Maeve's a good talker, but Mum's better. Once she gets started, there's no stopping her. 'So this pony is now trashing our flat,' she said. 'Filthy hoofmarks all over the floors, dung on the carpets, it'll be eating the curtains and wrecking the wallpaper, piddling all over the place – have you any idea of just how much a horse can pee? I tell you, they do gallons of it, we'll have it through the ceilings of the flat downstairs and the Council will be round, we'll get taken to court and fined. And what d'you think your dad's going to say?'

None of us wanted to think about that.

'Thank your lucky stars he's away, that's all,' Mum went on. 'But this horse is going out of here right now, and you have to get the place straight before you get any tea, I tell you, I'm locking the fridge.'

Our fridge doesn't lock, but I didn't say so. I didn't dare say anything.

Maeve cleared her throat nervously and said, 'He's not trashing *all* the flat, we shut him in my bedroom. With lots of straw. And there's vinyl on the floor, so it shouldn't go through to—'

Maeve's voice tailed off as Mum gave her a lethal look. The doors opened at the tenth floor, and we all got out. The other children had very sensibly stayed downstairs. Mum marched across to our flat, unlocked the door and went in. We followed.

It was an awful moment when Mum opened the door of Maeve's room. She stared in, and seemed too gob-smacked to say a word. We didn't say anything, either.

Rocket was lying on Maeve's bed, flat on his side, with his head on the pillow and his eyes blissfully shut. All four hooves were sticking out over the edge, and there was straw absolutely everywhere.

'Heaven help us,' said Mum faintly.

She put her hand to her forehead and shook her head slowly, and I thought for an awful moment she was going to cry, but she didn't. Rocket raised his head slightly from the pillow and blinked at her sleepily. He had a wisp of hay sticking out of his mouth.

'Did you ever see such a sight,' said Mum. She sounded sort of breathless. And then she started to laugh.

Maeve's duvet had pictures of galloping white horses printed all over it, and somehow that made the great, hairy shape of Rocket look particularly weird. Winnie giggled, and I found I was grinning, too. Maeve was still looking huge-eyed with fright, but Mum reached out and ruffled her hair and said, 'Sorry, darling. But honestly—' and then we were all laughing ourselves silly, Maeve as well.

When we'd calmed down a bit, Maeve said, 'I'm really sorry, Mum. But what could we do?'

Mum wiped tears of laughter away with the back of her hand and looked at Rocket again. 'We'll have to get him out of here by Saturday, though,' she said. 'Or your dad'll blow a fuse.' She turned to me and added, 'As to you, Dermot – the girls are totally insane, of course, but I never thought you'd go bats about a horse. Go and put the kettle on, there's a darling, we need a cup of tea.'

'If we're insane, then you are, too,' said Maeve, recovering her spirit. 'You were always saying about people in Dublin having ponies in their flats.'

'That's Dublin,' Mum said, as if it made all the difference.

From the kitchen, I heard the doorbell ring, and groaned. It would be the children again. This time, Mum went.

'Well, yes, we have,' I heard her say. 'He can't stay here, of course, but – do you want to come and see him?'

'Ooh, yes, please!'

A whole crowd of kids came in, more than there'd been before, giggling and squealing with excitement. The bell rang again, and it was another lot.

It kept ringing, and people kept coming in, grown-ups as well as children. I got down the big teapot. Mum came in and said, 'Dermot, can you nip to the shop for some biscuits? And some big bottles of Coke. Get as much as you can with this.' She fished in her purse and gave me a tenner.

*

By the time I got back from the shop, the flat was full of people. Rocket wasn't in Maeve's room any more – he was standing so close to the front door that I could hardly get in, and there were three small children on his back. Mrs Bardolini from downstairs was feeding him with lettuce leaves and Maeve was grooming his muddy tail with the bath-brush.

Mum always likes a party. She'd got going with the tea, and people were standing around with mugs in their hands, chatting and laughing and cooing over Rocket, and the kids were arguing about who was going to ride him next. We doled out Coke and put dozens of biscuits on plates, and a lot of them got fed to the pony.

More and more people kept coming in, and the place was absolutely jam-full. Two of the dads had found the model train lay-out in my room, and they'd got it going, so I had to keep an eye on them, to make sure they understood the points system. I don't like crashing the locos, it damages the rolling stock.

Mum came in with her mobile to her ear and flapped at the men and me to keep quiet. Then she made a face and said, 'Answerphone.' She listened, then spoke. 'Mrs Rix, it's about your pony. He's here. My daughter and her friend found him wandering, and they've rescued him. But he really can't stay here. Please can you ring me?' She gave the number, then switched off. 'She's out,' she said. 'I hoped she'd come round and get him, but the Lord knows where she is.'

'Looks like you're stuck with him,' said one of the men, coupling another coach to the loco.

'Does, doesn't it?' Mum agreed. 'We'll just have to hope Mrs Rix turns up, that's all. I wonder if they need some more biscuits out there.' And she went back to the bedlam in the hall.

There were shrieks, and Poppy Taylor ran in holding her nose and shouting, 'He's done another poo.'

I sighed, and Poppy ran out again.

'I like the signal-box,' said one of the men. 'Dead neat.'

We had a really good conversation about transformers and voltage reduction while the pony party raged on outside my bedroom door.

At last everyone started to drift off because it was getting late. Even the dads who liked trains went home.

'We might look in tomorrow,' one of them said. 'That OK?'

I said it was. They seemed quite sensible.

Maeve slept in my room, of course, on the top bunk. She trod on me several times, climbing down to see if Rocket was all right. And then climbing up again and whispering loudly that he was fine. Altogether, it wasn't much of a night.

CHAPTER 6

We were up hideously early the next morning.

'Got to do the mucking out,' Maeve said.

I could see what she meant. The state of her bedroom was truly awful. She got busy with the shovel then barrowed the stuff down in the lift, and when she came back, Mum was leading Rocket round and round our tiny hall because she said he needed exercise. I thought he'd get dizzy, turning in those small circles, but Mum said she kept changing him so he went the other way. 'Like they do in circuses,' she explained. 'They go anti-clockwise in the ring, then they have to canter clockwise afterwards, to unwind them.' I wasn't sure I needed to know this.

'It's Saturday tomorrow,' Maeve said. 'I'll take him out for a ride before Dad comes home. He'll be all right in the lift once he gets used to it.'

'Dad, you mean?' I asked.

Maeve aimed a pretend cuff at me, then went on, 'I could take him for a ride today, if I didn't have to go to school?' Her voice went up in a question. Nice try, I thought.

'You are going to school,' Mum said firmly. 'I've no intention of getting sued for having delinquent children, thank you very much. There'll be enough trouble about you taking the day off yesterday. And make sure your bedroom door is properly shut, right?'

''Course I will,' said Maeve.

The day seemed to go on for ever. I went to sleep in Literacy Hour, and there was a bit of a fuss about it. Maeve and Winnie were out of school like a flash when the afternoon ended, and sat thumping their fists on their knees because the bus was so slow.

Rocket was OK, but he'd eaten Maeve's curtains, or so we thought. Maeve burst into tears and said he'd die because horses can't digest curtains, but it turned out he hadn't eaten them, they were just buried in the straw and muck. I fished them up, and they were mostly there, only in several bits. So Maeve stopped crying.

'Poor darling, he must have been hungry,' she said, and gave the pony lots of hay and a pie-dish full of nuts.

Poppy Taylor was shouting through the letter box, 'Can I have a ride?' So she came in, and her little brother, then a whole lot more people.

Mum came home and put the kettle on. She was looking a bit worried. 'I don't know what's happened to Mrs Rix,' she said. 'I tried her from work every time I got a spare moment, but she's still not answering. I just hope she hasn't gone off for three weeks in Hong Kong or something.'

The men who liked railways turned up at that moment, so I took them into my room and left Mum to deal with the pony fan-club. The man called Ernie had a really good idea about a shunting yard. He'd drawn it on a bit of paper. I thought it would work quite well, so we started reorganising everything.

Then Mum rushed in with her mobile phone and kicked the door shut behind her to keep the noise out.

'Mrs Rix, thank goodness!' she said. 'I thought you'd gone to Hong Kong. What? Oh, Croydon, right...' She listened, then put her hand over the phone and mouthed at us, 'Two-day conference on knitted wall-hangings.' Then she went on, 'Listen, we've got your pony... You didn't know he was missing?' She rolled her eyes. 'Yes, well, I'm telling you, he is missing. He broke out of the field yesterday. Can you come and get him?' She listened. 'You don't drive. Oh. Can someone else... And you haven't got a horse box. I see.'

She gave me another cross-eyed look as if to say this woman is hopeless, then tried again. 'Do you at least have a halter? HALTER. Thing made of rope, to lead him by... You think so. That's something, anyway. Now look, can you bring it round here right away – yes, the halter. And get someone to mend the hole in the hedge, because... WHAT?' She pushed her fingers through her hair, making it stand on end. 'No, we *can't* keep him, this is a very small flat and there's barely room for... FLAT, yes. On the tenth floor. TENTH... Yes, tower-block, that's right.'

Mum listened for quite a few minutes. Then she took a very deep breath and said, 'OK, he belongs to your daughter and she's

71

not here, and you never wanted him. But, Mrs Rix, this pony now belongs to you. So can you please get round here with the halter, so we can lead him back to your place. Never mind about the hedge, we'll do something about it.'

I said, 'How?'

Mum gave me a huge shrug, then went on talking to Mrs Rix. 'I'll give you our address.' She spelled it out, very slowly and clearly, and explained several times how to reach us. 'See you soon, then,' she said, and held up crossed fingers to me as she switched the phone off.

Ernie looked up from a set of points and asked, 'A bit tricky, is she?'

'Totally bats,' said Mum. 'She doesn't know a thing about horses. The pony belongs to her daughter, who's gone to South Africa for six months. The silly girl told her mother it would be no bother, the pony would just live in the field, and as long as he had hay and water he'd be fine.'

Maeve came in at that moment, and overheard this. 'Mum, we can't let him go back there,' she said. 'Look, honestly, he'll be all right with us. I can take him down in the lift every day for exercise, and Dad will get used to him and—'

'You must be joking,' said Mum. 'I'm telling you, Maeve, this pony is not going to become a permanent lodger.'

'But, Mum—'

They argued their way out of my room and into the noisy hall, and I shut the door after them.

'We could have a siding behind the station,' I said, 'with a loop to connect back to the main line just past the curve.'

'Good idea,' said Ted.

The pony party was even bigger than yesterday's. People brought crisps and drinks and Mrs Bardolini came with an enormous pizza. Even Mrs Ebberly came, and took lots of photos, we weren't sure why. Anyway, it all got extremely loud and cheerful. Ernie and Ted and I took no notice. We were busy rebuilding the track, with a siding behind the station, like I'd said.

Then everything went very quiet.

It was a truly awful silence. I heard a little kid start to wail, and its mother said quickly, 'Ssh!'

I knew what had happened. There was only one explanation. My dad had come home from Spain. And this was only Friday night. He was early.

My hand froze on a set of points.

'Trouble?' said Ernie, and I nodded. Big trouble. It would have been nice to stay in my room, especially as we'd just got the new siding and loop to the main line operational, but I knew I'd have to go out there and do my bit. So I told Ted and Ernie, 'Just use one loco at a time until you've checked the track's all right. And don't go too fast, or they jump the points.' Then I went into the hall.

Dad wasn't shouting. In fact, he wasn't saying anything. He was just standing by the door with his zipper bag on the floor beside him and his arms folded. People were going out of the door very quietly. One or two of them said, 'Sorry,' as they passed him, but he just shook his head and looked patient. 'It's fine,' he said. 'Doesn't matter.' He didn't smile, though.

When they'd all gone, he nodded at the latest pile of poo that Rocket had done and said to Maeve and Winnie. 'Get that cleared up.' He took his phone out of his pocket, tapped in a few numbers and held it to his ear, and when someone answered he said, 'Police, please.'

'Oh, Dad, no!' Maeve was in tears and Winnie was looking terrified.

Mum put her hand on Dad's sleeve and said, 'Jack, don't you think we could—'

'Later,' said Dad. 'Hello? Yes, this is Jack Robinson from Flat 307, Greenview Towers. We have a small problem about a pony.' He walked into the living room, still talking. None of us followed him.

'I think I'll go home,' whispered Winnie. She made for the door but Maeve clutched at her and said, 'You can't! You've got to help me explain.'

'And clear up,' said Mum.

'But I haven't got the barrow,' said Maeve, 'it's downstairs with—'

'Never mind,' said Mum. 'Bung it in a bin-bag.' Someone rang the doorbell, and she added to me, 'Dermot, go and stand outside, and don't let anyone in.'

There were two children out there with their mum. I'd just got rid of them when some old bloke with a dog turned up. I told him he couldn't come in, but he argued. Said he used to be a donkey-man on a beach and he was an expert. I said donkeys were different from ponies, but he said that was rubbish, if you knew one you knew them all. Luckily Gammy Sam arrived at that moment. He and the donkey-man were friends, so after they'd grumbled a bit, they went off to the pub together.

When the lift came up again the runner-beans man got out, with his wheelbarrow, thank goodness. I told him to stick around because we'd have some more dung for him in a minute, and he said that was fine, he'd wait. He turned the barrow upside down and sat on it. I thought he might as well take over the job of keeping people out, since he was sitting there anyway, so I explained what was going on, and he said, no problem, he'd keep guard. So I went back into the flat.

Maeve and Winnie were scooping up the last of the muck using a folded cornflakes packet as well as the shovel, and Mum was in the kitchen, washing lots of tea mugs and Coke glasses. Rocket was shut in Maeve's room, but there was a thumping noise going on, as if he was kicking at the wall or maybe the door.

I took the bin-bag out to the runner-beans man, and he put it in his barrow. He was just going towards the lift when its doors opened and three police people came out, two men and a woman, all of them in uniform with yellow jackets over the top. The female one was quite young, and she wore a riding helmet and polished black boots. The men looked very big, with radios and truncheons and things bristling from their belts.

They walked past me and banged on the door of our flat and rang the bell. The runner-beans man gave me a sad look from the lift and said, 'That's the end of that, then. Still, thanks a lot.'

Dad took the police people into the living room, stepping carefully round Maeve and Winnie, who were scrubbing the hall floor. Mum came out of the kitchen, pushing a strand of escaping hair behind her ear, and asked if anyone would like a cup of tea. Nobody did.

The policewoman said, 'Where exactly is this pony at the moment?'

'In here,' said Maeve. She opened the door of her room and Rocket started to come out backwards, so she shut it again quickly.

'I see,' said the policewoman. She looked away and I thought she was trying not to laugh, but the policemen didn't smile.

We had to tell the whole story, and they wrote it all down. It took ages. They'd just about got to the end when the doorbell rang again, and Mum glanced at me.

'OK,' I said. My job is to keep everyone out. But as soon as I saw the woman who was standing outside I knew who she must be. She had untidy grey hair and she was carrying something made of knotted rope, with an end of it dangling down to her muddy feet.

'I'm Mrs Rix,' she said, 'I've brought the halter. Is this the right place?'

'Oh, yes,' I said. 'Come in.' And I took her into the living room.

She got a terrific telling-off from the policemen. They said it was an offence to allow livestock to wander on public roads, and she might be taken to court and fined. She said she didn't know about the hole in the hedge and she was really sorry.

'As to you girls,' the policeman went on, 'I can see you meant well, but another time, just phone us straight away, right?'

They both nodded. Winnie said, 'We never thought of it.'

Maeve asked, 'What's going to happen now? He can't go back in that field until the hedge is mended.'

'Of course he can't,' agreed the policewoman. 'We've got a horsebox downstairs. We'll take him to the police stables. He can stay there until we've made sure the hedge is secure and there's no risk of further escape.'

Mrs Rix looked unhappy. 'He'll have to

go,' she said. 'I can't cope with all this. I gave him some extra hay when I went to the knitting conference, but I'm not a horsy person. I find them rather alarming, to tell the truth. A horse stepped on my toe when I was small, and I never forgot it.'

'A riding school might buy him,' said the policewoman. 'He'd be better off there.'

Maeve was trying not to cry, but she couldn't help it. She managed to say, 'We'll never see him again,' then she was in floods.

'And we love him,' said Winnie. She was crying, too.

'Oh, dear,' said Mum. 'Such a shame. I know it's impossible here, we can't really spare a room as a stable, and there's the lift and everything, but he seems such a nice pony.'

I wasn't sure about that. It still sounded as if he was kicking at Maeve's bedroom door, or maybe knocking something to pieces.

'*Nice?*' Dad exploded. 'Just listen to him! Can we please stop talking and get this animal out of here before he turns the place into a total bomb-site?'

'Yes, of course,' said the policewoman, and stood up – but Mrs Rix had an idea.

'Maybe you girls could look after him for me,' she said.

Maeve and Winnie gasped. Then they shrieked, more or less together. 'Oh, YES!'

'We'll come every morning and every evening,' Maeve said, 'and—'

'Do you know anything about horses?' asked the policewoman.

Dad groaned and said, 'DO they! It's horses morning, noon and night in this place. They never talk about anything else. Been reading up about it for years.' Then he turned to Maeve and went on, 'I hope you realise that getting your room to rights is going to cost you every penny of your pocket money.'

'Yes, Dad,' Maeve whispered. This was not the time to argue.

Mrs Rix held the halter up untidily and asked, 'Do you need this?'

'Thanks,' said the policewoman. 'We've one in the Land Rover, but this'll do.'

She was very efficient with Rocket. She slid in beside him, slipped the halter over his head and backed him out of Maeve's room with no bother at all. 'Quite a good little chap, isn't he,' she said, though the room was pretty totally trashed.

'He's lovely,' said Maeve, opening the front door. Then she looked a bit wistful. 'What's it like at your stables? Will he get exercise and everything?'

'Of course he will.' The policewoman glanced at the men and said, 'We could let them have a look, couldn't we? Since they're so keen?'

The policemen shrugged. 'Up to you,' one of them said. 'We're not Mounted Division, that's your pigeon.'

'OK,' said the policewoman. She turned back to Maeve and Winnie. 'If one of your parents can bring you and take you back, I'll give you a quick tour.'

The girls gasped as if they'd been given the best Christmas present in the world.

'Mum, could we?' Maeve begged. 'Oh, please!'

Mum looked at Dad, and to my amazement, he said, 'All right, get your coats on. I'll take you.'

Maeve stared at him for a stunned moment, then she flung her arms round his neck and said, 'You're the best dad in the world.'

'Glad you've noticed,' said Dad.

Mum and I watched as the policewoman helped the girls reverse Rocket into the lift, then we went back to the flat. It seemed very quiet and empty, but in the silence, we both heard a quiet whirring noise.

Mum said, 'What's that?'

I knew what it was. In all the excitement, I'd forgotten about Ernie and Ted in my room. They were still in there, playing with the trains. I sighed, and opened the door.

'I think it's time you went home,' I said.

CHAPTER 7

The pony's real name wasn't Rocket, of course. He was called Jingle. The girls didn't seem to mind. They were so thrilled at seeing round the police stables, they both decided to join the Mounted Division as soon as they were old enough. The policewoman told them they'd have to pass their school exams, so they're working like mad, and Maeve gets up every morning when it's still dark to go and see to Rocket. Or Jingle.

They're off their heads, of course, but I'm quite glad it happened. Dad looked at me a day or two later and said, 'What about you? If you've got any mad ideas about what you want to do, you'd better say so now. It might save a lot of trouble.'

I said I'd really like it if we could go train-spotting sometimes. He didn't seem too keen, but he nodded and said, 'OK.' So if he's not away on a lorry somewhere he comes with me to Clapham Junction station on Saturday mornings. Last time we were there, I said, 'Trains are really sensible, aren't they. Not like horses.'

He didn't answer. But the Brighton Express was coming through and we were both looking at it, so I didn't expect him to. He's getting quite good about railways. And Maeve never says a word about moving to the country.

OTHER RED APPLES TO GET
YOUR TEETH INTO . . .

ANDREW MATTHEWS

Dido Nesbit is no ordinary girl – she's a Light Witch.
But being a modern day witch isn't easy – not when
you've got to juggle magic with schoolwork, friends
and all the usual problems a girl has to deal with.

Look out for the next two books in
The Light Witch Trilogy: *The Darkening* and
The Time of the Stars.

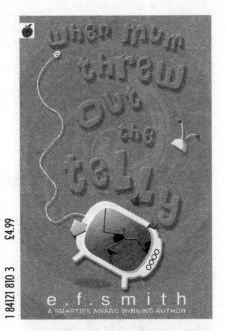

1 84121 810 3   £3 £4.99

EMILY SMITH

Jeff really liked television. Cartoons were more
interesting than life. Sit-coms were funnier than life.
And in life you never got to watch someone trying
to ride a bike over an open sewer. Sometimes at night
Jeff even dreamed television. Mum complained, but
it didn't make any difference. Jeff didn't take any
notice of her, which was a mistake.

A very funny and thought-provoking book from
Emily Smith, winner of two Smarties Prizes.

1 84121 456 6   £4.99

CHRIS D'LACEY

David soon discovers the dragons
when he moves in with Liz and Lucy. The pottery
models fill up every spare space in the house!

Only when David is given his own special dragon does
he begin to unlock their mysterious secrets
and to discover the fire within.

Inside the illustration:
Do Not READ Any Further

£4.99

1 84121 456 6

Finch's secrets on boys
Cringeworld
Sleepovers
Best Friends...
As revealed only to Pat Moon.

PAT MOON

Loads of secret stuff about BOYS, worry bugs,
babies, enemies, etcetera, etcetera.
Snoopers will be savaged by Twinkle
(warrior-princess guinea pig).

Also by Pat Moon:
Do Not Read This Book was shortlisted
for the Sheffield Book Award

MICHAEL LAWRENCE

Something's after Jiggy McCue! Something big and angry
and invisible. Something which hisses and flaps and stabs
his bum and generally tries to make his life a misery.
Where did it come from?

Shortlisted for the Blue Peter Book Award

'*Hilarious.*'
Times Educational Supplement

'*Wacky and streetwise.*'
The Bookseller

MORE ORCHARD RED APPLES

❏ *The Fire Within*	Chris d'Lacey	1 84121 533 3
❏ *The Darkening*	Andrew Matthews	1 84362 188 6
❏ *The Time of the Stars*	Andrew Matthews	1 84362 189 4
❏ *When Mum Threw out the Telly*	Emily Smith	1 84121 810 3
❏ *The Poltergoose*	Michael Lawrence	1 84121 836 7
❏ *The Killer Underpants*	Michael Lawrence	1 84121 713 1
❏ *The Toilet of Doom*	Michael Lawrence	1 84121 752 2
❏ *Maggot Pie*	Michael Lawrence	1 84121 756 5
❏ *Do Not Read This Book*	Pat Moon	1 84121 435 3
❏ *Do Not Read Any Further*	Pat Moon	1 84121 456 6
❏ *How to Eat Fried Worms*	Thomas Rockwell	1 84362 206 8
❏ *How to Get Fabulously Rich*	Thomas Rockwell	1 84362 207 6

All priced at £4.99

Orchard Black Apples are available from all good bookshops,
or can be ordered direct from the publisher:
Orchard Books, PO BOX 29, Douglas IM99 1BQ
Credit card orders please telephone 01624 836000 or fax 01624 837033
or visit our Internet site: www.wattspub.co.uk or e-mail:
bookshop@enterprise.net for details.

To order please quote title, author and ISBN
and your full name and address.
Cheques and postal orders should be made payable to
'Bookpost plc.' Postage and packing is FREE within the UK
(overseas customers should add £1.00 per book)

Prices and availability are subject to change.